B55 088 673 X

D1585606

PiZAZZ

VS EVERYONE

Read more from the
SUPER world of

Pizazz
Pizazz Vs The New Kid
Pizazz Vs Perfecto
Pizazz Vs The Demons
Pizazz Vs Everyone

PIZAZZ VS EVERYONE

IT'S NOT EASY BEING SUPER...

Sophy Henn

SIMON & SCHUSTER

First published in Great Britain in 2022 by Simon & Schuster UK Ltd

Text and illustrations copyright © 2022 Sophy Henn

This book is copyright under the Berne Convention.
No reproduction without permission.
All rights reserved.

The rights of Sophy Henn to be identified as the author and illustrator of this
work has been asserted by her in accordance with sections 77 and 78
of the Copyright, Designs and Patents Act, 1988.

1 3 5 7 9 10 8 6 4 2

Simon & Schuster UK Ltd
1st Floor, 222 Gray's Inn Road
London
WC1X 8HB

www.simonandschuster.co.uk
www.simonandschuster.com.au
www.simonandschuster.co.in

Simon & Schuster Australia, Sydney
Simon & Schuster India, New Delhi

A CIP catalogue record for this book is available from the British Library.

PB ISBN 978-1-3985-0583-4
eBook ISBN 978-1-3985-0584-1
eAudio ISBN 978-1-3985-0585-8

This book is a work of fiction. Names, characters, places and incidents are either
the product of the author's imagination or are used fictitiously. Any resemblance
to actual people living or dead, events or locales is entirely coincidental.

Printed and bound by CPI Group (UK) Ltd, Croydon, CR0 4YY

MIX
Paper from
responsible sources
FSC® C171272

Rotherham Libraries	
B55 088 673 X	
PETERS	21-Mar-2023
	6.99
CHILD	RTMAL

MEET THE SUPERS ...
my mum
AKA ATOMIC
my dad
AKA ORE
my ANNOYING Little Sister
AKA RED
DRAGON
Wanda
1/2 dog 1/2 telephon

Grandma
AKA RAY
Gramps
AKA INFERNO
AUNTY BLAZE
SHE'S SO COOOOOOL
Uncle Teaser
Uncle Titano-OOOOO
Jett
my super friend
Granny
my secret baddie friend
Aunty FURY
KAPOW
UH-OH

... AND THE NORMALS

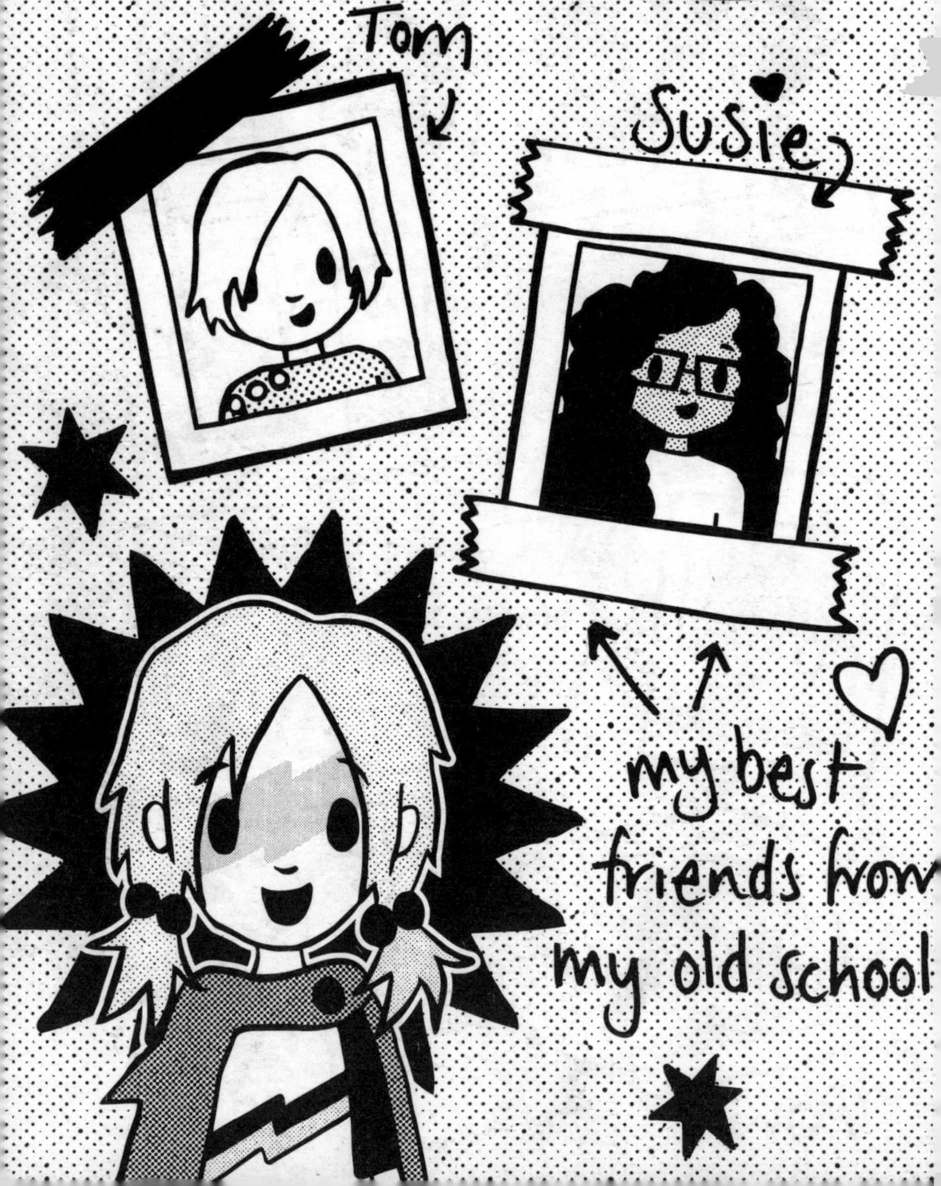

The bit where I explain myself . . .

Hi.
   My name is **Sarah**,
and I live a **totally NORMAL life** and
NEVER have to wear a TOO-BIG cape
and fight

SUPER
BADDIES
EVER.

Ha-de-ha-HAAAAAAA.

I WISH!

Actually, my name is **PIZAZZ**,
my life is *completely* weird,
I **DO** have to wear a TOO-BIG cape
and I **DO** have to fight *SUPER BADDIES*
ALL THE TIME.
And with the most embarrassing
SUPER POWER.

EVER.

This is because I am . . .

A SUPERHERO!

The rest of my family are all

SUPERHEROES

too and boy do they LOVE it.

Like, **REALLY** LOVE it.*

But I don't. In fact, I'm not even sure I slightly like it. Sometimes I just wish I was a NORMAL person and didn't have to worry about **PLANETS** being knocked off their axes,

intergalactic warlords getting the hump or a *SUPER SNEAKY BADDIE* filling the world's supply of gel pens with invisible ink so we all have to do our homework TWICE. EYE ROLL

I **would** like to be *SUPER* at **ROLLER SKATING**, though – that would be *brilliant*. Obviously.

*Except for *Aunty Fury*, my dad's *BADDIE* sister. She went to the dark side because she clearly **didn't** love it either.

If I am *completely* honest there are a few **GOOD** things about being a *SUPERHERO*. Not many, but a few . . .

UmmMMM...

Well...

Oh, OH,
FLYING... *

*Oh yeah, and **SAVING** the **UNIVERSE** and stuff.

UH-OH . . .

I nearly f**o**RG**o**t to mention **WANDA**, which could have *something* to do with the time I was hit on the head with a **LLAMA** (long story) and I am almost certain THAT is the reason I f**o**RG**e**t loads of things all the time. Or it could very *easily* be because **WANDA** is always sneaking about under my feet and t**r**ip**P**i**n**g me up.

And that's not all she does,

OH NO.

She's also a sort of *telephone*, receiving messages from **Mission Control** about **SUPERHERO** missions we have to go on and any other important **SUPERHERO** business we need to know about. And I hate to admit it, but she does do excellent SIDE-EYE, too.

SIDE-EYE

You might have thought that being a **SUPERHERO** who has to ZOOM OFF all the time to save the **UNIVERSE** was more than enough for a 9¾-year-old to be getting on with. But NO, it turns out that **SUPERHEROES** have to go to **school** on top of all that. Mum says it's just in case we *finally* defeat all the **BADDIES** and have to do something other than *WHIZZ* about with our *LASERY*, fiery, SPEEDY **SUPER POWERS**. I always snort-laugh when she says this because . . . YEAH, RIGHT!

I WISH!

If I have learned **anything** from this **SUPERHERO** business it's that there is **ALWAYS** another **BADDIE** just waiting to step in and cause havoc. It's like a **SUPER BADDIE** vending machine that **NEVER** runs out; one drops down and another moves *FORWARD* to take their place.

sigh

There are **_BADDIES_** in my **normal life** too, but instead of **_SUPER-BADDIE_** powers, they use stuff like WORDS and SNIFFY faces to be **MEAN**. And even though they are kind of **MEAN**, somehow everyone still seems to LOVE them.

Er, have you like seen her shoes? They are SO last year.

And you will NEVER believe what she said . . .

But it's NOT **ALL BAD**.
There are *goodies* in my life as well . . .

★ **SUPER** ONES: My ridiculous *family*, I suppose.

EYE ROLL

★ **BADDIE** ONES: I KNOW!
I have two **SECRET BADDIE** friends – KAPOW
and Perfecto – because *sometimes* this **SUPER**
business isn't as **black** and white as the
movies make it seem.

SAVE WATER...
NO.
MORE.
BATHS.

NO
MORE P.E.
TO SAVE ENERGY

★ **NORMAL ONES**: I have some especially GOOD *goodies* as my school friends. Ivy, Molly and Ed and I have been through all sorts together AND we are in a BAND, AND we are the school **ECO COUNCIL** – trying to turn the school green. Well, not *actually* the colour green; that would be ridiculous . . . OR would it? Hmmₘₘₘₘₘ. I might put that in our **ECO SUGGESTION BOX** . . . We get some quite '*interesting*' suggestions from time to time . . .

RECYCLE <u>ALL</u> SCHOOL REPORTS <u>BEFORE</u> THEY GET SENT HOME.

BE MORE ENERGY EFFICIENT . . . WALK EVERYWHERE VERY SLOWLY. ESPECIALLY TO DOUBLE MATHS!

So that's me, **PIZAZZ**, ECO COUNCIL member, Lead Guitarist/Singer in **The Cheese Squares**, frequent **nerd**, collector of **BLACK NAIL VARNISH**, good **friend**, IRRITATED big sister, *guinea-pig* soulmate, EYE-ROLLING **daughter**.

AND
RELUCTANT
SUPERHERO,
whether I want to be
or **NOT**.

2

The bit where Gramps gets poorly . . .

When I got home from school I was feeling **almost** like a **WINNER**. Well, maybe that's going a bit far, but I definitely didn't feel like a **Loser**. So that was sort of a **WIN**!

I had defeated Harry the Slime almost **SINGLE-HANDEDLY** before school AND I only got HALF covered in slime (unfortunately it was the TOP half) . . .

Nothing particularly **embarrassing** had happened during the rest of the day (unless you count **Ricky Owens** standing on my cape so that when I went to go to maths I got **yanked** back to history instead). **Mum** was cooking tea so I was extremely **CONFIDENT** that it wasn't going to be one of **Dad**'s mouth-burning **CHILLI** surprises (the surprise being there is more **CHILLI** in it than ANY OTHER ingredient!) and I wasn't face first on the floor like I so often am when **WANDA** is sneaking about **tripping** me up. So basically . . .

RESULT!

BUT THEN . . .

I was in such an *averagely* good mood that I even said hello to Mum when I walked in, but when Mum replied it wasn't with a JOLLY 'HELLO!' like normal, and she didn't look even slightly happy. But she didn't look **cross** or *disappointed* or a bit miffed, either. These are her TOP **four** faces, so I was *struggling* to work out what she WAS looking like . . . then I realised she was **SAD**. I wasn't used to this face on Mum and it made me feel all UNComfortable.

Mum sat me and my annoying little sister, RED, down and told us Gramps was in the hospital. He had been *trying* to get rid of a plastic bag that had blown up into one of the trees in the park next to school when he caught himself on a branch. He had then got into a bit of TANGLE, fell and **hurt** himself. This was the park that Gramps had helped me and Ivy SAVE from being turned into a car park.

He liked it
SO much he'd *decided*
to look after it now he was
retired from being a

SUPERHERO.

Anyway, Mum said he
was going to be fine,
but it had made him
go a bit Wibbly
and also a bit glum.

So obviously then I got a bit **glum** too. Then I got **cross**. **Gramps** is my *favourite* family person by about a **MILLION** light years, and it really wasn't at all fair that he had hurt himself while picking up other people's rubbish. The thought of him being Wibbly AND **glum** was just too horrible. **Gramps** is NEVER **glum** – in fact, he is LAUGHING almost eighty-seven per cent of the time. Then I got a bit **WORRIED** because what would happen if **Gramps** did start LAUGHING

in hospital? I asked **Mum** if **Grandma** had taken in her portable **fire extinguisher** to put out thc little **trumpy fireballs** he makes if he laughs TOO much, but **Mum** said not to **WORRY** as the hospital had put special **fire-retardant** sheets on his bed and he was wearing his special reinforced pyjamas. Then we had a **LITTLE LAUGH**, just WITHOUT **fireballs**.

Mum promised that we could go and see **Gramps** after dinner, and that cheered us all up a bit. Then she said it was **MushROOM oMeLeTTes** for tea and that made us all **SAD** again.

I went to get my best friend and spiritual guide, BERNARD, from her (yes, HER!) cage so we could talk it all over. BERNARD is a *guinea pig*, hence the cage. Well, she's sort of FIVE *guinea pigs* now as there was a bit of an 'accident' with **SUPER BADDIE COPYCAT**'s wonky SuperPower Duplicator™ laser gun and I 'might' have zapped my *guinea pig* into FIVE *guinea pigs*. But it all worked out OK in the end, because now they have formed a *vocal harmony group* (all except STINK-EYE, who just, well, looks STINKILY at **everyone** ALL the time)

and I feel fairly certain they will be a worldwide **SENSATION** any time now and, as their owner/manager, I will obviously become rich, rich, RICH!

BERNARD THE FIRST agreed about it being SUPER **UNFAIR** that **Gramps** was in hospital thanks to someone else's littering. I could tell this from the way she was thoughtfully NIBBLING the corner of the card I was making for him. I had *decided* to make him a *get-well-soon* card because I didn't know what else to do. I knew it wouldn't *actually* make him better, but I was hoping it would cheer him up, even a little. I was just using my jazz hands/glitter storm **SUPERPOWER** to add some sparkles to the card (I mean, no one has ACTUALLY said I can't use it for that) when **WANDA** walked in.

Of course she did. EYE ROLL

She jumped onto my bed, rolled around in the duvet, did that funny wiggly thing dogs do on their backs, flipped over, licked her paw and then told me I had a **MISSION** to go on and to get in the kitchen for a briefing RIGHT NOW!

I felt all wrong about going on a **MISSION** when **Gramps** needed me, and it made me **CROSSER** than I usually am about it. Plus, I really didn't like to leave the card half finished and HALF EATEN by BERNARD. But of course I didn't really have choice as **SUPER BADDIES** don't tend to wait around for me to finish craft projects.

As I ran out, I made BERNARD *promise* she wouldn't EAT the rest while I was gone. I think she understood . . .

NIBBLE NIBBLE

T WELL

SO I GUESS THAT'S A NO TO MY FIRE-BREATHING SKILLS, THEN?

WELL, TOXIC GOO AND LASERS ARE JUST TOO RISKY . . . KABOOM!

MOLTEN METAL IS PROBABLY A NO-NO TOO, THEN?

AHHH, LET ME GUESS . . . IT'S DOWN TO ME AND MY NON-FLAMMABLE GLITTER STORM?

GET OUT OF MY WAY, PIZAZZ!

AS MUCH AS I WOULD REALLY LIKE TO DO THAT, I'M AFRAID I CAN'T. MY MUM WOULD BE FURIOUS!

FINE!

FINE!

SPLAT

SPARKLE!

MMMNPF!

FFFFFFFUNPHHH!

ARRRGH!

WHAT?!? AM I ACTUALLY GOING TO WIN THIS?

DOUBLE SPLAT!

I'M OUTTA HERE!

THE CLEAN-UP BEGINS AND POWER IS RESTORED . . .

ACME GEL glitter pens

THE END

SPOILER: IT'S NOT!

On the way home I realised that it was too late to go and see **Gramps**.
Stupid **SAVING-THE-WORLD** had ruined
EVERYTHING.
AGAIN.

The five **BERNARDS** must have sensed my disappointment as when I went to bed they all rallied round and sang me a '*soothing*' song to help me feel better. Well, all except **STINK-EYE** who just looked on . . . **STINKILY**.

It didn't really work, but I *appreciated* the effort.

3

The bit with
Aunty Fury . . .

When RED woke me up I felt a bit better, but then my brain woke up and it remembered all about **Gramps** and how it was **BEYOND UNFAIR** that he was stuck in hospital for trying to right someone else's wrong. And a silly, pointless wrong at that – there were plenty of bins in the park, and if that litter bug had just used one of them then **Gramps** wouldn't be in hospital. I started to feel a bit **cross** about it all over again, **so cross** I couldn't eat my **CHEERY FLAKES** as they were far too, well, **CHEERY** . . .

AND THEN **WANDA** WALKED IN

AGAIN!

WHAT NOOOOOWWW?

BUT, AUNTY FURY, RUINING WORKS OF ART BY MAKING THEM LOOK ANGRY IS WRONG!

ERM, THAT'S SORT OF THE POINT! WHAT DO YOU THINK, PIZAZZ?

PIZAZZ TRIES TO THINK OF SOMETHING . . . ANYTHING . . .

ERRRM . . .

. . . BUT SPOTS AN ANGRY PICTURE AND GETS THE GIGGLES INSTEAD!

A-HA! YOU DO FIND IT FUNNY!!!

KNEW IT.

ERRR, NOPE.

ABSOLUTELY NOT. AHEM.

I ALWAYS SUSPECTED YOU WERE A BIT ON THE BAD SIDE, PIZAZZ . . . IF YOU EVER DECIDE TO COME OVER TO THE DARK SIDE, YOU KNOW WHERE I AM!

GULP.

Fighting **Aunty Fury** had made me feel a bit **uncomfortable**. Aunties are for chats, shopping and basically being like your **mum** except **not** *completely* EMBARRASSING.

They are **NOT** for suggesting you become a **BADDIE** and go to **THE DARK SIDE**. But before I could really have a proper think about all that it was time for school.

I was still *trying* not to feel **cross** about Gramps or funny about \ **Fury** when I got to class. I went and sat next to **Ivy**, like usual, but not like usual **Ivy** was looking quite sad.

When I asked her why, she told me that the **ECO COUNCIL**'s campaign to save the school *pond* hadn't worked – the governors were still going to fill it in and put more parking spaces in its place. I couldn't believe it! We had put up posters ALL OVER SCHOOL telling people how great the *pond* was, we'd done an **ASSEMBLY** about it (with costumes), we'd done a *presentation* for all the grown-ups about the **ECO SYSTEM** (including the *pond*, OBVS) and written a song about it (as The Cheese Squares) called '*SATURDAY NEWT FEVER*'. Surely now everyone had to *understand* how important the *pond* was?

How could they even consider **filling it in** after ALL THAT?

AND **REPLACE IT** WITH **CARS?**

When I said all this to Ivy she stopped looking sad and said that we mustn't give up and that we must plan a **Pond Protest** immediately. While I really wanted to be as *focused* and positive as Ivy, I just couldn't help feeling **FURIOUS**. Why wasn't looking after the planet something that EVERYONE wanted to do? We all have to live here,* so why on EARTH don't we **ALL** look after it?

First **Gramps** hurts himself picking up someone else's litter and then Ivy gets **SAD** because after trying her BEST to do the right thing, the people that were *supposed* to know better had shown that they very much didn't.

I **STOMPED** off to class wondering why anyone **BOTHERED** doing **anything**. EVER.

* Erm, well, technically I don't HAVE to live here as I can *ZOOM OFF* to wherever I want, but all my FRIENDS are here and I haven't seen a **ROLLER DISCO** on any other planet so I would really rather stay.

The rest of the day was pretty **average**.
Well, if you are ME, that is . . .

Accidentally
**GLITTER
STORMED**
Mrs Harris

**Tripped
over
CAPE**

By the time I arrived home I'd cheered up a bit, because I *remembered* that we were going to see **Gramps** later and I could take him the card I had made. Well, the half BERNARD hadn't EATEN.

As I lay on the floor in the hallway, after tr**i**p**P**i**ng** over a sneaky **WANDA**, she told me about a **mission** I had to go on. I tried to explain that I couldn't as I had to visit **Gramps** and give him his card, then after that I had to make the posters I had promised **Ivy** for the **ECO COUNCIL**'s **Pond Protest**, but **WANDA** just scratched her ear and looked bored. So I told her I knew that **saving the planet** was important and all that, but couldn't someone **else** do it, just this once? But then she just said NO and *wandered* off.

FINE.*

* Definitely NOT fine.

COOEEE! COOEEE! COOEEE! COOEEE! COOEEE! COOEE

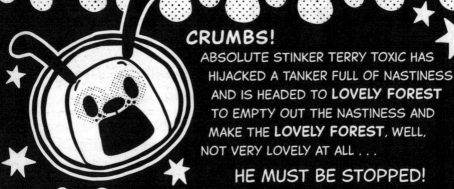

CRUMBS!

ABSOLUTE STINKER TERRY TOXIC HAS HIJACKED A TANKER FULL OF NASTINESS AND IS HEADED TO **LOVELY FOREST** TO EMPTY OUT THE NASTINESS AND MAKE THE **LOVELY FOREST**, WELL, NOT VERY LOVELY AT ALL . . .

HE MUST BE STOPPED!

THAT EVIL BADDIE TERRY TOXIC IS DRIVING THE HIJACKED TANKER . . .

. . . FULL SPEED TO LOVELY FOREST.

SOMEONE MUST STOP HIM BEFORE IT'S TOO LATE.

OUR HEROES ZOOM IN . . .

MWAHAHAHAHAAAAAA!!!

CLUNK

ATTACH HOSE HERE

LOVELY FOREST WILL BE YUCKY STINKY FOREST IN NO TIME!

MEANWHILE, IN LOVELY FOREST...

...IT'S LOVELY. REALLY LOVELY!

NOT FOR LONG!!!!

HOORAY! OUR HEROES HAVE ARRIVED!

NOT SO FAST!

PUT THE HOSE DOWN!

LEAVE THE FOREST ALONE!

WHAT THEY SAID.

BUT THE NASTINESS IS TOO POWERFUL...

OOPS.

QUICK, PIZAZZ! GRAB THE HOSE...

SIGH

SWITCH IT OFF!

SPLAT!

ER, HELLO! ANYONE?

PIZAZZ! IT'S OFF NOW...

ER, THANKS.

AND LOVELY FOREST IS SAVED!

BUT MY HAIR ISN'T.

OBVIOUSLY by the time **Mum** had **POWER HOSED** the **gunk** off me it was TOO LATE to go and see **Gramps**. Or start the **Pond Protest** posters.

The bit where
I go . . .

THE NEXT DAY . . .

I felt a bit **SICK** in the car on the way to school the next morning, and I was almost *positive* it wasn't because of the THREE bowls of **CHOCO POPS** mixed with **FROSTY FLAKES** and secret packet of prawn-cocktail crisps I had just eaten, but *actually* because I was worried about **Gramps**. Then I remembered I hadn't learned my spellings or made the posters for the **Pond Protest** either and felt a bit **SICKER**.

When I got to school I saw **Ivy**, Molly and Ed by the entrance, but I just couldn't face telling **Ivy** that I'd let her down, posterwise, so I snuck round the edge of the playground (not at all easy with a GIANT, FLAPPY SHiNY CAPE with my **name** across the back) and into the side entrance. Then I used one of my other **SUPERPOWERS** –

DAWDLING.

I'm starting to think it's *possibly* the **SUPERPOWER** I am **best** at (but I am almost certain I would NOT want to be called

DAWDLE GIRL
or THE DAWDLER

or even DAWDLE-A-TRON)

and slipped into the tutor room right at the last minute so I didn't have to talk to anyone.

After **Mrs Harris** took the register, we all filed out and **Ivy** asked me if I was OK. 'Er, NO, not really – constantly trying to **save the planet** feels *completely* EXHAUSTING and NEVER ENDING and sometimes *totally* POINTLESS and occasionally **SOGGY**' was what I wanted to say, but I didn't. Instead I just said, 'FINE!' in that *special* way that clearly means I am **NOT** and then I felt **BAD** and apologised for not doing the posters for the **Protest**.

By lunchtime, **Ivy**, Molly and Ed had asked me what was **WRONG** about 136 times and while I knew they were only worried it didn't help at all. In fact, all it really did was remind me that **everything** felt a bit **WRONG**. So when **Ivy** said we HAD to have a meeting about the **Pond Protest** after school something went **POP**.

I knew it shouldn't have,

but it just sort of did . . .

and not in a **FUN**, **fizzy PoP** way,

more of a

CROSS, **ANGRY PoP** way.

71

Why did I have to sort out EVERYTHING? **BADDIES**, litter, **POSTERS**, homework, **ponds**, spellings, **toxic gunk**, **saving the planet**... it was ENDLESS. There was always *something* else to **save** or sort out, no matter what I did. And look at **Gramps** – he had spent his whole life **saving the planet** and did anyone appreciate it? NO! They just dropped their litter in the park for him to pick up and now he was in the hospital. In the hospital WITHOUT a slightly *chewed*/EATEN card from me.

I really, *really* did my BEST to **save the planet**, even when I didn't *particularly* want to, but no matter what I did it just **NEVER** seemed to be

ENOUGH.

I tried to shake the not *particularly* great feeling all day, but I couldn't. So when I wasn't **shaking** I was **STOMPING**. I figured if I looked and sounded **GRUMPY** enough, no one would BOTHER me and right now I did NOT want to be **BOTHERED**.

Then at the end of the day, I **SNUCK** out of the side entrance of school again to AVOID the other **ECO COUNCIL** members. I just wanted to be on my own and not have people telling me what else I had to do. Anyway, I was sure they could cope without me and my *non-existent* POSTERS. Really, what *difference* did I even make?

As I was leaving, I saw **Ivy**, Molly and Ed putting up **POSTERS**. Posters about the **Pond Protest**. So I guess I really didn't make that much *difference* at all; they were clearly fine WITHOUT me.

FINE.

FINE.

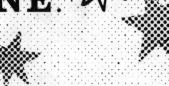

When I got home, I went to my room in my new **STOMPY-DO-NOT-BOTHER-ME** way. I *super* hoped it got the message across because I had decided to sneak out before dinner to see KAPOW (one of my secret **SUPER BADDIE** friends). I was so tired of trying to do the **right thing** all the time and getting exactly NOWHERE, I just really needed to talk to someone who didn't have to get things **RIGHT**, like,

EVER.

TOMP   STOMP   STO

Before I could even think about sneaking off, **WANDA** lolled into my room. She clearly hadn't picked up on my new '**GO AWAY**' vibe. In fact, quite the opposite – she walked over and started scratching herself by rubbing her back against my legs as she told me we had a **Mission** to go on.

REALLY?

NOW?!

EYE ROLL

UH-OH!!

THAT TUNEFUL SCAMP THE TERRIFYING TENOR HAS DECIDED TO USE HIS VOCAL SKILLS TO MAKE THINGS EXPLODE AND HIS FIRST TARGET IS THE BEAUTIFUL STATUE OF PEACE IN PRETTY TOWN. STOP HIM AND KEEP PEACE IN ONE, ERM, PIECE. PLEASE!

OUR DASTARDLY BADDIE IS WARMING UP HIS VOCAL CORDS . . .

OOOOOOHH

ME ME MEE

BBBRRR

READY FOR HIS BIG MOMENT . . .

OUR HEROES ARRIVE . . .

AND MAKE A PLAN . . . BUT WAIT . . .

PIZAZZ SPOTS A LITTERBUG . . .

AND NOW SHE'S MAD . . .

HOW DARE HE HURT GRAMPS!!!

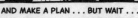

ER, WAIT A MINUTE, IS PIZAZZ CROSS WITH THEM OR LITTER IN GENERAL?

LINDED BY HER FURY, SHE
AKES A RUN-UP AND . . .

OOOOOOH NOOOOO . . .

KNOCKS THE PEACE STATUE . . .

HEY, GO AND PICK UP YOUR LITTER!

SMASH

THAT'S SORTED. NOW FOR THE STATUE . . .

YOU WERE SUPPOSED TO SAVE IT, NOT SMASH IT!!

MUM EXPLAINS WHAT HAS JUST HAPPENED . . .

PIZAZZ!! HOW COULD YOU?

OH NO, AND THE TERRIFYING TENOR IS STILL GOING STRONG . .

AHEM.

T WAIT . . . RED HAS AN IDEA . . .

AND TICKLES HIM SO HE CAN'T SING!

AHHH . . . RED HAS SAVED THE DAY . . .

OF COURSE SHE HAS

sigh

Well, I suppose I should be used to being shown up by my ANNOYING little sister by now, but actually BREAKING something I was *supposed* to be **saving**? That was a new low. And Mum was clearly *disappointed*, even if she did say sorry for getting **cross**, so I still felt **AWFUL**. It didn't help that everyone was *congratulating* RED on **saving the day** . . . I mean, I did too – she did do a GOOD job (even if she is totally IRRITATING) – but all that just made me feel double **USELESS**, especially as I had already let **Ivy** down today. And the rest of **THE ECO COUNCIL**. And all the *frogs*. And the *newts*. Not to mention the *goldfish*.

sigh

I'd messed up. And when I mess up, **SUPER**-wise, it's a **proper BIG mess**. Like, REALLY big and everyone knows about it. I really do *try* to get things right, and I really do *want* to get things right, but there's just always SO MUCH to get right. And no matter how hard I try, I seem to just get so much **wrong**. Maybe it was time to admit I am no good at **saving** things, fancy *statues* or **ponds.** Maybe I am just a *BAD SUPERHERO*.

Then I remembered what **Aunty Fury** had said the other day. Maybe she had a point – what if I was better suited to being a *BADDIE*? Maybe if I was a *BAD SUPERHERO* that actually meant I would be a **GOOD SUPER BADDIE**. That sort of made sense, maybe. And **Aunty Fury** certainly seemed HAPPY, not *constantly* feeling BAD about not being, well, *BAD* enough. So when no one was looking I sneaked off to see **KAPOW** . . . what if I really had had enough of all this **world-saving** business? Maybe I was tired of feeling *BAD* for messing up when I was *actually* trying my best . . . maybe it was time for a change. **A BIG CHANGE** . . .

5

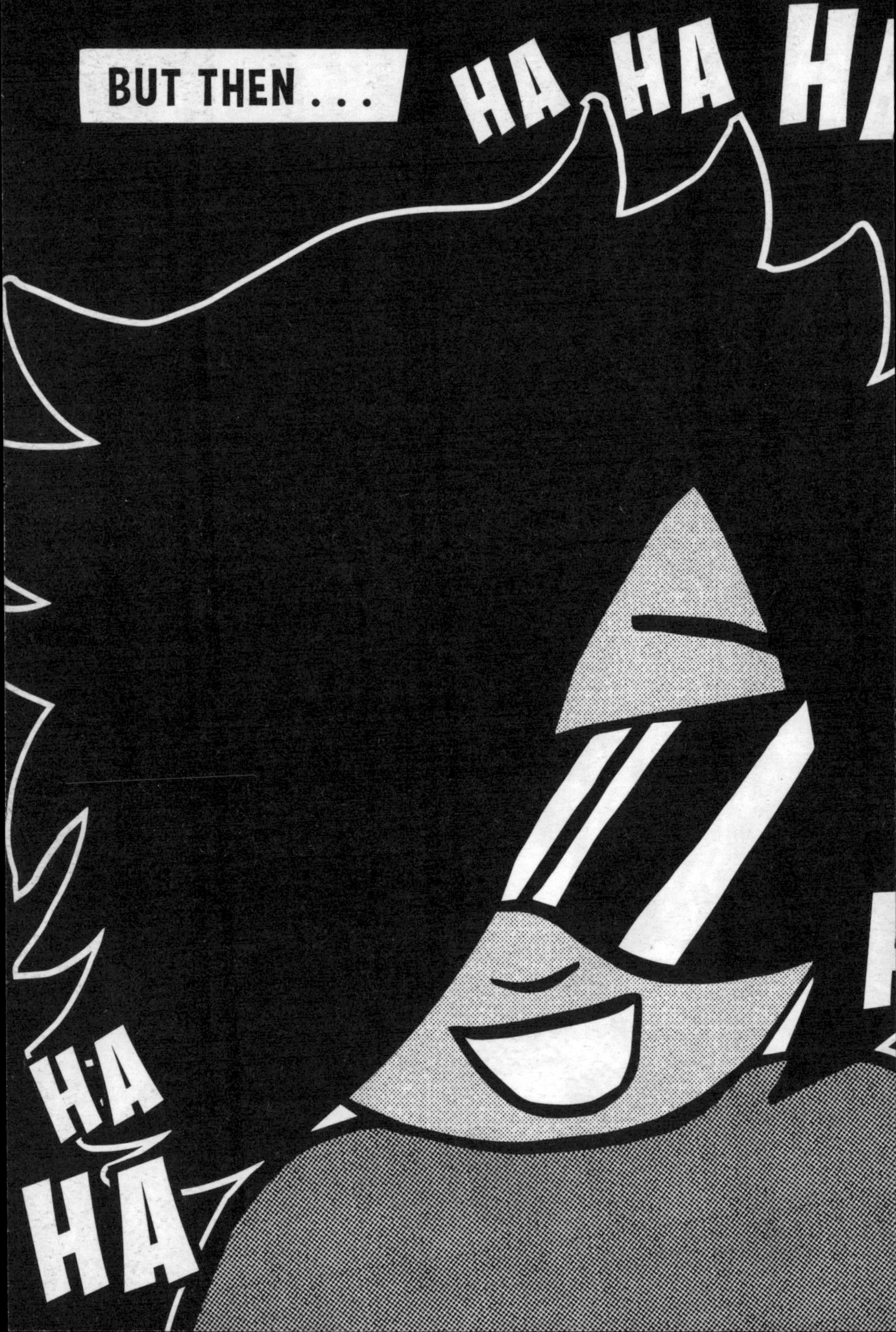
BUT THEN . . .
HA HA
HA
HA

KAPOW didn't exactly react to my announcement that I was *considering* becoming a **BADDIE** *quite* as I had expected him to.

Once he had stopped **LAUGHING** and once I had convinced him I WASN'T joking (that took quite a while) he asked me why on earth I would want to do that?

So I *explained* that being a *goodie* was super HARD and everyone expected you to always **save the day** . . . **EVERY. SINGLE. TIME.** Because you were the *goodie*, you had to care about EVERYTHING and EVERYONE, which meant when you did mess up it felt *completely* and extremely **HORRIBLE**. And there was always another calamity just around the corner.

And you still had to do the same amount of homework as people who DIDN'T have to **save the world**, which was hardly fair.

Being a **BADDIE** was clearly far easier as no one ever *expected* you to succeed. In fact, they ALWAYS hoped you **FAILED**, and you didn't have to really care about anything because how could you if you were *constantly* threatening to **MUCK STUFF UP** all the time?

And YOU could decide when and where you wanted to be **BAD** and not have to race off after *goodies* the whole time.

KAPOW pointed out that even if you were a **BADDIE** you still had to do homework.

Oh well, it couldn't be all *good*.

Or was that **BAD**?

But mainly **KAPOW** looked super surprised and said this didn't sound like me at all and I said well, maybe this had *actually* been me all along. It's not like I have ever really loved being a **SUPERHERO** and I seemed to be pretty **RUBBISH** at it – what *difference* do I really make? Other than actually SMASHING the things I was supposed to be **saving**, getting dunked in **toxic goo** and **FIGHTING** my own aunty. Maybe I should just leave it to **SUPER** *goodie-goodie* RED to do all the **saving** and I can just bob about being a bit **BAD**.

Then **KAPOW** started **LAUGHING** again. WHAT? Was it really that hard to imagine me being a double **SUPER BADDIE**?

Apparently so.

So when **KAPOW'S** dad SHOUTED up the stairs that it was his turn to threaten to mess up a small town, I decided this was the perfect *opportunity* to show him just how **BAD** I could be . . .

My first **BADDIE** mission . . .

92

OUR NEWLY BAD HERO IS READY TO RUMBLE . . .

ER, GUYS!?! WHAT'S GOING ON? PIZAZZ, WHAT ARE YOU DOING?

I'M BEING **BAD**!!! GOOD, ISN'T IT?

WE ARE GOING TO MESS NEAT TOWN RIGHT UP!

IT REALLY PLAYS TO MY STRENGTHS. I AM GREAT AT BEING MESSY!!!

AND THAT WAS ALL THE ENCOURAGEMENT OUR HERO, I MEAN BADDIE, NEEDED . . .

PIZAZZ!!!

YOU'RE **BAD**?!?

I'M SO PROUD!

PICKING NEAT FLOWERS, MESSING UP NEAT HAIR, RUINING NEAT DOG'S DOS!

PIZAZZ! STOP! BEING BAD IS NOT AS FUN AS YOU THINK. I'D RATHER BE GOOD, TO BE HONEST!

DON'T TELL MY MUM.

WHAT ARE YOU TALKING ABOUT? THIS IS GREAT!!!!!

WE'VE GOT **BADDING** TO DO! . . .

THAT'S MY GIRL! NOW COME WITH ME, PIZAZZ . . .

UH-OH . . .

QUITE A LOT LATER . . .

It was exciting at **Aunty Fury**'s. I mean, there is the SHARK TANK for starters, and she doesn't mind how many **snacks** you eat before tea, or if you eat your greens – BECAUSE SHE'S A **BADDIE**. In fact, she is **so BAD** she just ordered **pizza** for tea – ON A **WEDNESDAY** – and we didn't even have to eat the crusts.

I wasn't supposed to visit her – Dad said she was a **BAD** influence (DUH!) – but now I was kind of a **BADDIE** too it was EXACTLY the sort of thing I should be doing, right?

We talked a lot about annoying little sisters. **Aunty Fury**'s is **Aunty Blaze** who was apparently just like RED when she was younger. A super-achieving, happy, shiny **SUPERHERO**, and Grandma and Gramps *completely* adored her. **Aunty Fury** said she never really felt like she exactly fitted in and was certain she would NEVER manage to be like **Aunty Blaze** no matter how hard she tried. This got her wondering if she was actually *supposed* to be a **SUPERHERO** at all.

Then when **Gramps** was lost on a **Mission** in another galaxy, **Aunty Fury** got really cross. She had asked **Mission Control** to send her out to look for him, but they had refused. Er, what was the point of being a **SUPERHERO** if you couldn't save the people you loved? And when she tried to talk to **Grandma** about it everything went a bit wrong. It all turned into a **GINORMOUS** argument with **Grandma** defending **Mission Control** . . .

WHAT? And that's when **Aunty Fury** got SO **FURIOUS** she walked out on **Grandma**, **Aunty Blaze** and Dad, and decided to become a **BADDIE**.

THEN THERE'S THE FACT YOU DECIDE *WHEN* YOU WANT TO BE **BAD**. NOT LIKE WHEN YOU ARE A GOODIE AND HAVE TO *ZOOM OFF* TO DEFEAT **BADDIES** . . .

. . . SO, REALLY, I GUESS US BADDIES *GET* TO DECIDE WHEN *GOODIES* HAVE TO BE *GOOD* TOO! HAH!

Then I realised the time, and even though I am a bit of a **BADDIE** now I am still only 9¾.

So I had a bit of a panic and **Zoomed** home.

ACTUALLY QUITE LATE . . .

When I snuck back into my room it was all nice and quiet so I quickly went to my desk to *pretend* to do some homework, all the while thinking about how much fun I was going to have being a *BADDIE*. But for some reason my stomach seemed to disagree with these thoughts and was **FLIPPING** about all over the place. And NOT in good way. But then my new *BADDIE* senses kicked in and I stopped thinking about my stomach/being a *BADDIE* and I started to wonder if *everything* was a bit too quiet. Where WAS everyone?

I couldn't even hear THE BERNARDS singing, but I COULD feel the power of STINK-EYE's STINK-EYE, and sure enough there she was GLARING at me. Was it my *imagination* or was she GLARING at me HARDER than she did usually? Did she **know**? Surely she couldn't object to me being a *BADDIE* . . .

she was called STINK-EYE!!!

I was so busy being *completely* distracted by STINK-EYE that it was extra super *surprising* when, all of a sudden, Mum, Dad, RED and Aunty Blaze all burst into my room. RATS! I had known something was up and I had been RIGHT . . .

Aunty Blaze explained that apparently some tattletales had called **Mission Control** and told them they had spotted me with KAPOW and Perfecto. So obviously I started to wibble a bit, which turned into a **PANIC**,

then my tummy stopped flⁱppⁱng and started to **PANIC** too and I was feeling **very** fuⁿny indeed.

What was I going to say?

What was my TUMMY going to say?

I tried to remember everything I had talked about with *Aunty Fury* and THEN I remembered that I didn't CARE any more, not now I was a **BAD *BADDIE***. I had no business feeling wibbly, **PANICKY** or even **GURGLEY** because now I was ***FIERCE*** and ***HEARTLESS***. So I stood up and told everyone . . .

I AM NOW A *BADDIE*.

Just like **KAPOW**, their response WASN'T exactly what I had expected, or even hoped for. But then I just figured, well, *of course* that's how they will react . . . I was the one who ALWAYS **messed things up**, I was the one who had a CAPE that was **too long** for her and I was the one that EVERYONE else **LAUGHED** at.

Well, we'd see who would get the last laugh.

Me.

It would be **me**.

Or possibly
 THE BERNARDS.

But hopefully **ME**.

 ME.

When
everyone
had FINALLY
stopped laughing
they got up to leave.
PRIVACY AT LAST.
Just as Mum was about to
shut the door, she turned and
told me that **Gramps** sent his love –
apparently they had stopped by the
hospital on the way home.

Right at that moment I felt so **SUPER
CROSS** I couldn't even move. Why had they
gone without me? Why didn't they tell me?
If they had told me I wouldn't have snuck off
and I would have seen **Gramps**.

ARRRGGHHH!

Mum shut the door and then suddenly my **CROSSNESS** came shooting out of my legs and I **ZOOMED** around the room. When most of the **CROSSNESS** had *disappeared* I just lay on my bed and practised being **FEARSOME**. It really did take an awful lot of concentration and made me quite exhausted.

Eventually THE BERNARDS turned up. Apparently they had been out to a costume fitting for their first live tour. And no, I didn't ask because now I didn't care.

But I did wait until they were all asleep and then did a little **LAUGH** to myself.

I GOT IT!

The last **LAUGH**.

HA!

Oh, another one!

6

When I woke up extra early I couldn't help but smile, and I was almost positive it was a slightly **EVILER SMILE** than usual. Well, I decided, I had a lot to **EVIL SMILE** about . . . I was now a **SUPER BADDIE**, which would mean a new costume, which would mean one that my mum wouldn't chose for me. I was positive that **BADDIES** didn't let their mums choose their clothes. Or maybe they did, then they'd refuse to wear them and pick the exact OPPOSITE to wear instead. WOW!

This was all

VERY EXCITING.

While my wardrobe was rather limited (literally the **EXACT SAME OUTFIT** over and over) I decided to DESIGN a costume using some stuff I reckoned I could get my hands on . . .

SLIGHTLY EVILER ME
DANGEROUSLY SPIKY HAIR
SLIGHTLY HARPER EARS
DASTARDLY EYEBROWS
SNEAKY SMILE
POINTIER SHOULDERS

Then I started to have a **THINK** about all the ways I could be **BAD** in my day-to-day life too . . . but when I shared my ideas with **STINK-EYE**, I *realised* I needed to up my game a bit as she DIDN'T look even *slightly* IMPRESSED, in fact her eyes were almost **UNSTINKY**.

PIZAZZ'S LIST OF EVIL DOINGS:

Return my library books at least two days LATE.

NEVER turn the lights off EVER!!!

Leave the LIDS off my PENS
(oh, and the toothpaste).

Put my dirty washing on the FLOOR.

Ditto WET TOWELS.

Drag my feet.

Pick my NOSE as often as possible
(preferably in front of people).

Put my ELBOWS on the table.

School could not go fast enough because

1. It's SCHOOL;

2. I couldn't wait to get home to make my new *BADDIE* costume and show *Aunty Fury* and;

3. It's SCHOOL.

Annoyingly Ivy cornered me at tutor time and asked if I was OK. What was wrong with everyone? I was **VERY** OK. I mean, apart from my stomach feeling like a washing machine, swirling and *SWOOSHING* around, I WAS FINE. I explained to Ivy that I was no longer a fairly **rubbish SUPERHERO**, but the far more enjoyable option . . .

I was now a *SUPER BADDIE*. And if I was now a *SUPER BADDIE*, mainly focused on **NOT CARING** about stuff and **DesTROYing** things, it seemed a bit silly being on the **ECO COUNCIL**, which was mainly concerned with **caring** about stuff and **saving** things.

Besides, I didn't seem to be very good at being a **SUPER** *goodie* or an **ECO COUNCIL** member anyway. I wasn't sure I had really made any *difference* to anything, **POSTERS** or otherwise, so maybe this had all worked out for the BEST.

Ivy said that I made a LOT of difference . . .
I had co-founded the **ECO COUNCIL** with her and
how would we have **saved** the park next to
school from Mr Piffle and his **BIG BUSINESS**
without my jazz hands/glitter storm?

I almost FORGOT I didn't care for a minute
as **Ivy** had a good point and then I felt a bit
AWFUL. Then I remembered I was **tired**

generally **messing things up** and for all the school **frogs** about to lose their home. I was always trying my **best** and getting things **WRONG** then feeling *BAD* about it, so I had now decided to not even **bother** to try. That way I wouldn't keep DISAPPOINTING everyone, including me. Now I would **mess things up** on purpose and have **FUN** doing it. So I told **Ivy** I had already decided. And also that maybe this was the best opportunity I would ever get for a new costume, so really **that** was **THAT!**

As soon as I got home I got busy on my new costume. It was a *good* way to **distract** myself from thinking about how hurt Ivy looked earlier. Not caring took A LOT of effort and I had to keep reminding myself that now I was on **THE DARK SIDE** I didn't care, I DIDN'T care, I DIDN'T CARE!!!

I *might* have said this **OUT LOUD** because RED stuck her head round the door and asked **what** I didn't care about and I just yelled **EVERYTHING** and threw a book at the door.

Which felt GREAT for about a nanosecond, but then I felt a bit **HORRIBLE** for being, well, **HORRIBLE** again, which didn't bode well for my new *BADDIE* status. So I concentrated on trying to copy STINK-EYE's STINKY-EYED look. I think I got pretty close, which just seemed to make STINK-EYE STINKIER.

Ha!

I'M SO BAD!

After dinner, which I just pushed around my plate while looking **cross** because (and I'm not sure if I have mentioned this) I was now *BAD*, Susie called. **Susie** is one of my two BEST friends from my old school (the other one is **Tom**) and she is the most *SUPER* person I know at giving advice. She is **BRUTALLY** honest, and that's why I was almost certain she wouldn't approve of my new *BAD* self,

so I told **Mum** I was busy with homework and congratulated myself on also adding **LYING** to my list of *BADDIENESSES*.

While I was pleased I was breaking into **NEW** areas of *BADDIENESS*, **LYING** to Susie made my tummy feel funny again and it didn't feel like a GOOD type of funny. AGAIN. But I decided to ignore it . . . All *BADDIES* probably had funny-feeling tummies, right?

I needed something to distract me from my funny-feeling tummy so I decided to **ZOOM** over to *Aunty Fury*'s evil lair to get her opinion on my new *BADDIE* costume. After all, she was the ONLY one who seemed to 'get me' these days. I thought it was coming along very nicely . . . Well, considering what I had to work with.

When I got there *Aunty Fury* put me through my *BADDIE* paces . . .

EVIL LAUGH (NEEDS WORK)

TELLING PEOPLE MY EVIL PLAN BEFORE DOING IT

FINALLY *Aunty Fury* seemed to think I had the **BADDIE** thing down and so I suggested we go out and

BE

BAD...

When I snuck back in – SURPRISE –
Mum was sitting on my bed with THE BERNARDS
and they all looked VERY huffy indeed.
Normally this would have made me **SUPER**
worried, but now I was a ***BADDIE***, this sort
of situation was what I **LIVED** for . . .*

* Not so much my
stomach, mind you . . .
GURGLE

It turns out that you can still get told off and **NO sweets** for a WHOLE week if you are a *BADDIE*. Then Mum asked me **where** I had been . . .

Erm,

WHERE have I been?

I have been

BEING BAD!!!

EYE ROLL

AND THEN IT HAPPENED . . .

AH AHA HA
A HA HA!

My FIRST properly EVIL,

EVIL LAUGH.

Mum got up and left and took all THE BERNARDS back to their cage and I was all **alone**. I saw a note on my desk saying that **Susie** had called again, but I REALLY didn't want to talk to her – I didn't want to *hear* what she thought of my NEW *BADDIE* status.

Anyway, all this me-time was GREAT! I could do what I wanted, I didn't have any **ECO COUNCIL** business to worry about, no time-consuming phone chats with **Susie** and **Tom** and *certainly* no tiring trips to see KAPOW and Perfecto. Yeah, this was **REALLY GREAT**.

Really, REALLY

GREAT?

But then I realised that all this down time was the perfect *opportunity* to turn my bedroom into my very own **EVIL LAIR**. All the GOOD **BADDIES** had one, after all. It was . . .

DASTARDLY MAKEOVER TIME . . .

7

The bit where I go fully BAD . . .

Mum and Dad were still **GRUMPY** with me for **sneaking** out. And **RED** was **GRUMPY** with me for . . . Well, who cares? Not me, ooooh NO. Or maybe they were all just **startled** by my radical **new** LOOK . . . **WANDA** even started to **retch** when she first saw it, but that could have been down to her trying to eat a **sock**. WHOLE.

Anyway, I didn't want them to LIKE it, I didn't want **anyone** to like it. I didn't even really like it, if I was honest, but that WASN'T the point. I was *BAD* and now I looked *BAD* too. But not *BAD* like AWFUL, *BAD* like EVIL. Ish.

My new outfit caused quite the commotion when we got to school. I mean, even if you didn't **see** it you could certainly *HEAR* it – bin liners are very *RUSTLEY* (NOTE TO SELF: make a quieter version as this one is **NO GOOD** for sneaking). *EYE ROLL*

Ivy, Molly and Ed certainly looked **surprised** when I arrived at our tutor room, and Mrs Harris just did that very, VERY high eyebrow look she does, like they are almost **zooming off** the top of her head. Ivy asked if I had changed my mind about the **ECO COUNCIL** and I pointed out that as I was dressed TOP to TOE in **plastic** bin

liners, did it look like I had **CHANGED** my mind?

Then she asked if they were **BIODEGRADABLE** and I said **NO** and that I had *deliberately* chosen them because **why NOT**?

And then Ivy told me all the **reasons** why not and I started to feel a bit like I WAS caring again so I went and sat over the other side of the classroom, the *BAD SIDE*. Well, the side where Serena and The Populars usually sat so *BADDISH* . . . I think Serena even gave my slightly NOISY but mainly COOL new look an admiring glance.

As we left for our first lesson, **JETT**, the other **SUPER** in my class, cornered me and asked me what on **EARTH**, **JUPITER** or even **MARS**, I **LOOKED** like?

So I told her that I obviously looked like a **BADDIE** and that was because I had decided to go to **THE DARK SIDE**. This must have rattled **JETT** as she *involuntarily* hovered up off the floor and she asked why on **EARTH**, **JUPITER** or even **MARS** I would do that?

I told her that actually being a **BADDIE** was **easier** and more **FUN** and the outfits were **COOLER**. CLEARLY! She said she had to agree that my new outfit was **COOLER** than my usual outfit (er, thanks?) but that working hard was not a **BAD THING** and it actually made it feel all the better when you achieved what you wanted. But then she **would** say that because not only is she REALLY **good** at being **SUPER**, she is also **REALLY GOOD** at sport, so says stuff like that all the time.

I just yawned which I hoped showed **JETT** that I was:

a) tired of WORKING HARD and;
b) tired of **talking** about WORKING HARD.

JETT just looked **cross** and walk/hovered away. I couldn't believe how easy this being **BAD** business was . . . I was a **NATURAL**. All I had to do was keep ignoring the not-nice, funny feeling in my tummy and I would be FINE.

Serena and The Populars came over to check out the **NEW BAD ME**.

Serena was all like 'So you're, like, BAD now, huh?' and I was all like 'Yeah, I guess I, like, TOTALLY am?' and then Serena was all 'Yeah, but you can't just, like, *decide* to be BAD and

say you are' and I said, 'Like, obviously. **EYE ROLL**
Everyone knows that.' So I asked **Serena** when
was the last time she 'like, totally TRASHED
PLUTO' **EYE ROLL** and **Serena** had to say 'Like
NEVER' because obviously she has never
even been to the **MOON** let alone **actual**
PLUTO. And I *decided* that there was really no
need to say whether I actually HAD TRASHED
PLUTO or not (NOT).

 Then I *think* **Serena** actually looked
slightly impressed. Slightly. Then she asked
if I 'Like, wanted to hang
out?' and so I said
(and this *surprised* me
too) I would 'Like,
think about it'.
And off I
 RUSTLED.

SAY WHAT?!?!

Even I was *surprised* that the **NEW BAD ME** didn't **care** about hanging out with **Serena**. Old me obviously WOULDN'T have wanted to, what with being GOOD and having friends like **Ivy**, Molly and Ed, but **old** me would've also been a bit *secretly* excited that **Serena** was being something other than totally **MEAN** to me. And I really thought **NEW BAD ME** would have wanted to be friends with the **MEANEST** girl in school. It was all very confusing and my tummy was *clearly* trying to tell me something, but I wasn't really in the **mood** to listen as I was **FED UP** of being told what I should be doing by EVERYONE including my own stomach, so I kept *ignoring* it. I was better on my **own**, doing what I wanted, **NOT caring** about ANYTHING or even

ANYONE.

I decided to show *everyone* just how much I really DIDN'T **care** for the rest of the day . . .

(This was a bit PAINFUL . . .)

(This was EXTREMELY **messy**, so it's a good job my new costume is WIPE CLEAN.)

The last one *actually* got me into **TROUBLE** and I was told I had to go to the HEAD TEACHER's office after school . . .

EYE ROLL

I might have *slightly* **cared** as I was walking down the corridor to the HEAD TEACHER's office at home time, but I did my best NOT to let it show, even if my knees gave it away. Then when I saw Mum was sitting in the HEAD's office my **face** might have *slightly* given it away too.

DISAPPOINTED

SURPRISED

It turned out that my **NOT caring** had been very much noticed and this had made everyone *disappointed*. Also *surprised*. And a bit **cross**. I wasn't at all sure **WHY** they were surprised. I mean, LOOK AT ME!!!! And I was used to being *disappointing* (I mean, the **POSTERS** for Ivy, the fancy *statue*, the general uselessness), but I wasn't very keen on the **crossness**. Then I figured that's just a side effect of being a *KICKIN' BADDIE*, and so I concentrated on **NOT caring** again.

CROSS

The bit
where
I end up
by my
(BAD)
self . . .

The car ride home with Mum and RED was **SUPER** *quiet* (well, apart from my costume RUSTLING).

It was so *quiet* you could actually **feel** the *quiet* filling the car and it felt REALLY **HEAVY**.

When we got home, I was braced for a proper **TELLING-OFF** from Mum, Dad, maybe **WANDA** and possibly even **RED**, but everyone just got on with their after-school business as usual . . .

RED – doing her spellings and pruning her **BONSAI** trees.

Mum – doing whatever it is mums even do . . . probably **eating chocolates** and reading magazines.

Dad – making MORE **CHILLI** and **WANDA** – organising her half-eaten sock collection – **AHHHHH** so that's where the ODD socks go . . .

For someone who is actually rather **snooty** she has VERY questionable habits . . .

Mum said they were going to go and see **Gramps** again later and asked if I wanted to go. Well, OBVIOUSLY.

But I wasn't at all sure I wanted **Gramps** to see me *BAD*; he was such a **BRILLIANT** *goodie*.

The thing was I couldn't NOT be *BAD* now – I had told EVERYONE. I got all confused and felt a bit Wibbly again, and

then the Wobbles were threatening to come out as **tears** and I couldn't let this lot see me CRY (it didn't go with my new image AT ALL), so I sort of shrieked, '**NO!**' and **STOMP**/ **RUSTLED OFF** to my room.

AGGGHHHHHHHH...

Everything was *completely* WEIRD. I mean, I had been the **BADDEST** I had EVER been today (AND I had been trying pretty hard!), so why WASN'T everyone **SHOUTING** at me? Or **BANNING** me from things (Dad LOVES **BANNING** things!) or SOMETHING?

ANYTHING!

As I sat on my bed I decided, quite firmly, that I really, *definitely* didn't want to see THE BERNARDS or Ivy, Molly and Ed. I *certainly* didn't want to talk to **Susie** or even **Tom** and I very much did not want to see KAPOW, he was being far too *good* (ER, CONFUSING).

And I *absolutely* DID NOT want to see **Gramps**, OOOOOOH NO! I just wanted to be BY MYSELF and not have to worry about being a good *guinea-pig-super-band-manager*/**ECO-COUNCIL MEMBER**/friend/**SUPERHERO**/whatever.

On my own I could just think up **new ways** to be *BAD*. *BADDER* than *BAD*. Yup, that was *definitely* what I wanted to do.

ALL. ON. MY. OWN.

When **WANDA** came barrelling into my room to tell me about a **Mission** we had to go on, I tried to explain that I couldn't *possibly* go as technically I was now on the **other side**, so sending me was *actually* no HELP at all. In fact, quite the **opposite**. But she just **COUGHED** up most of a sock, gave me some side-eye, flicked her **ears**, turned around and PRANCED out. **WOW! COUGHING** up a **sock** and still remaining the snootiest being in the room –

IMPRESSIVE.

HE'S . . .

EFT ALL THE LIGHTS ON . . .

MIXED UP THE RECYCLING . . .

AND EVEN . . .

SMUSHED ALL THE PLANTS . . .

VERYTHING IS SUCH A MESS . . .

. . . WHERE WILL OUR HEROES START ???

I'LL SHUT THE LIGHTS DOWN!

I'LL ORGANISE THE RECYCLING!

AND I WILL SAVE WHATEVER PLANTS I CAN, THEN RE-POT THE BROKEN ONES AND PLANT SOME NEW ONES. THEN LEARN MY SPELLINGS!

AND PIZAZZ? . . .

TO BE CONTINUED . . .

TO BE CONTINUED TOO . . .

The bit where Gramps makes **A LOT** of sense . . .

AS USUAL.

It was actually quite **BORING** at **POLLUTOOOO**'s **EVIL LAIR**. They didn't even have a **SHARK TANK**. Or a telly. It wasn't like **Aunty Fury**'s at all. In fact, it made her spikey cave lair look positively **cosy**. It was also very **uncomfortable** on account of every surface being covered with **rubbishy JUNK**, which made sitting down quite PERILOUS.

NO! NO! NO!

NICE-FREE ZONE

RUBBISH RULES OK?

I thought about my **nice**, *comfy*, but also **UTTERLY DASTARDLY** though far **less smelly** room at home and my tummy had that funny feeling again. Then I tried VERY hard to stop thinking about *home* because THIS was what I wanted – **freedom**, *FUN* and **less HASSLE**. Yes, THIS WAS GREAT...
Mmmmm. **Great**.

BUT THEN . . .

All of a sudden **POLLUTOOOO**'s dad came in and was all **SHOUTY** and **cross** with **POLLUTOOOO** for **MESSING UP**. I even sort of felt **BAD** for **POLLUTOOOO** as it didn't seem at all **nice** and *definitely* not even slightly **encouraging**. Then he yelled that **POLLUTOOOO** should go and make up for it by diverting a waste pipe of **toxic nastiness** into a *lovely lake* of *loveliness* and **MUCK IT UP**. **POLLUTOOOO** looked pretty **embarrassed** but asked if I wanted to come too.

I tried to sound very **COOL** and fairly disinterested and replied that we should *absolutely* go and do that, partly because I was fighting an **extreme URGE** to start tidying up (WHAT?!? Tidying up was NOT something **BAD BADDIES** did! I didn't even do that when I was **GOOD**) but mostly because I wanted to get away from **POLLUTOOOO**'s scary dad. I also said **yes** because what else could I do? The **ECO COUNCIL** would hardly take me back now I was hanging out with someone called **POLLUTOOOO**. I had been super **MEAN** to my own sister, **IGNORED** my oldest friends' calls and not **even** been to visit my *lovely* but poorly **Gramps**. I guess I really was **BAD** now and *everyone* knew it. Other than **Aunty Fury**, the only person I had to hang out with as of five minutes ago was a **BADDIE** with a really **SHOUTY** dad. I didn't exactly have a LOT of options.

POLLUTOOOO said we should FLY OUT *immediately* – there was **no time** to (**toxic**) WASTE . . .

ER, YEAH, OF COURSE. SO, ER, WHERE'S THIS PIPE OF NASTINESS, THEN?

OUR BADDIES LOOK FOR THE PIPE HIGH . . .

. . . AND THEY LOOK LOW . . .

NTIL FINALLY . . .

SAVE OUR PIZAZZ!

GRAMPS!

ER, PIZAZZ . . . WHO'S THE OLD MAN AND WHAT DOES HIS SILLY SIGN SAY?

GRAMPS, WHAT ARE YOU DOING HERE? SHOULDN'T YOU STILL BE IN HOSPITAL?

PIZAZZ, HOW COULD I NOT COME? RED TOLD ME ALL ABOUT IT AND IT SOUNDS LIKE YOU ARE IN A BIT OF A PICKLE.

I KNOW THIS SUPER BUSINESS CAN GET TOUGH SOMETIMES, BUT THIS ISN'T YOU, PIZAZZ, NOT REALLY.

IT'S TOO LATE. I DON'T THINK ANYONE LIKES ME ANY MORE.

IT'S NEVER TOO LATE TO SAY SORRY . . . OR ADMIT YOU GOT IT WRONG.

AND WE ALL HAVE OUR MOMENTS, PIZAZZ. YOU AREN'T THE FIRST SUPER TO HAVE A WOBBLE AND YOU WON'T BE THE LAST.

COME ON, PIZAZZ!

WE'VE GOT TO GET A MOVE ON OR MY DAD WILL BE FURIOUS!

WE'VE GOT A PIPE TO DIVERT AND A LOVELY LAKE TO MESS UP!

FORGET THE OLD YOU, AND LET'S GET IT DONE!!!

gulp

GURGLE

SAVE OUR PIZAZZ!

ARRRRRRGHHHHH!

ZOOM

IT'S ALL SO CONFUSING! WHAT AM I SUPPOSED TO DO?

POLLUTOOOO IS MY ONLY FRIEND NOW.

BUT GRAMPS...

OH, HELP!

As **Gramps** and I sat on some **MOON ROCK** and looked back down at the Earth, I told him **EVERYTHING**. **Gramps** just listened like he always does and then *reminded* me that I had made so many **DIFFERENCES** already . . . by helping to **save** the park next to school **AND** by defeating **LOTS** of *SUPER BADDIES* **AND** by being a **GOOD** friend **AND** by managing a premier *guinea-pig vocal*

harmony group AND by being one of the two best granddaughters ever AND by making the **BEST** half of a _get well_ card he had **ever** seen (ʀᴇᴅ took it in apparently). He said that you can make a **BIG** DIFFERENCE sometimes and you can make a sᴍᴀʟʟ **DIFFERENCE** sometimes. You can even make a **medium-sized DIFFERENCE**, but they all add up.

And **THAT**'s what **counts**.

Gramps also said that *sometimes* I am going to get it **right**, and *sometimes* I WON'T, and it works that way for everyone. It NEVER changes, no matter how **BIG** or **old** or *SUPER* you get. And that's OK. But what is **not** OK is letting your mistakes define you. **Gramps** said you have to let them **teach** you instead. You see, EVERYONE get things **wrong**, but those **wrongs** turn into **rights** if we *learn* from them and then let them go.

And then he told me to STAND UP so he could have a proper look at my **BADDIE** costume, so I did. He **LAUGHED** so hard he made almost **ONE HUNDRED** little trumpy **fireballs**, but as there is no atmosphere on the **MOON** they immediately went out and **Gramps'** trousers were only slightly **SINGED**.

Phew!

10

The bit where I realise some stuff . . .

POLLUTOOOO was absolutely **FUMING** I had gone back to the **GOOD** side, but I honestly didn't really care what she thought. **Gramps** had helped me with that.

In actual fact, **Gramps** had helped me with a LOT of things. So many things. **All the time**. And what had I done? **DRAGGED** him out of his poorly bed to come and STOP me from being a **TOTAL idiot**. I felt **AWFUL** and I couldn't stop saying **sorry**, but **Gramps** just gave me a **HUG** and told me that that was what being a *goodie* was all about. You couldn't choose when you got to help people – you could be needed at any time – but it was **always**, **ALWAYS** the RIGHT thing to do. If someone needed your **help**, you gave it to them. Then when YOU needed **help**, someone would

be there for **YOU**.

When we got home Ivy, Molly and Ed were there waiting with Mum, Dad, Grandma and RED, and I had never been so **pleased** to see all of them, **EVER**. I said **sorry** to everyone OVER and OVER and told Ivy that the plastic bin liners **were** actually **BIODEGRADABLE** after all, I just PRETENDED they weren't, then we had a RUSTLEY **HUG** and I finally let out all my Wibbles. Then I told her that I would make sure I **helped** all I could to **save** the **pond**, and Ivy asked me if that meant I was back on **THE ECO COUNCIL**. I asked if I was **allowed**, and she said she'd had to ask her **CO-FOUNDER** then she asked ME if I was *allowed* back on and I said

YES!

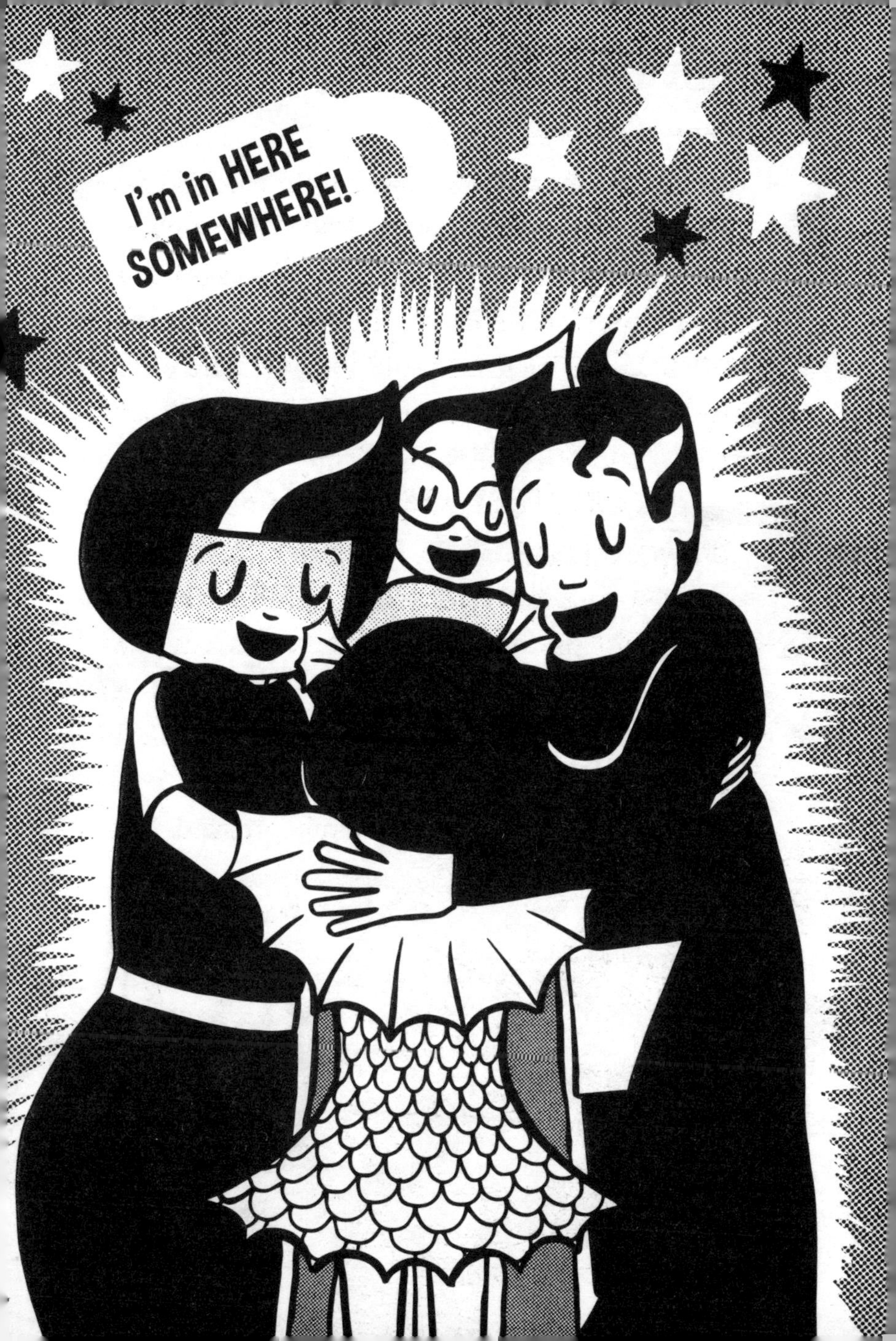
I'm in HERE SOMEWHERE!

After I went and got changed, Mum made us all some sweet tea, **Gramps** declared we should **CELEBRATE** my return from **THE DARK SIDE** with a nice BIG dinner and Dad suggested **CHILLI**. Obviously. So we all yelled 'NO!' (but NOT in a nasty way) and Mum ordered **pizza** instead. But *assured* us we would **definitely** have to eat the **CRUSTS**.

I suddenly realised I was **SUPER** hungry, probably because my tummy had FINALLY STOPPED feeling so funny and now felt like having some **pizza** in it.

Aunty Blaze and Uncle Titanooooo had stopped by too and we were all having a *lovely* time when the **doorbell** went. I couldn't imagine WHO it could be as pretty much everyone was here except for **Granny** who was on a *spa break* and **Uncle Teaser** who was on a **STAND-UP** tour of Australia. But the **bell** went AGAIN, so I couldn't have *imagined* it (in your face, **LLAMA**) and I left the table to answer the door.

Once we had all got over the **SHOCK** of:

a) Aunty Fury coming to visit;

b) an actual **SHARK** at the door and;

c) finding out **SHARKS** like *pizza*,

Aunty Fury explained she had had enough of being a **BADDIE**. She told us it was really very **lonely**, which was why she was so HAPPY to help **me** become a **BADDIE** so I could keep her company. But when she had seen me go a bit **BAD** it made HER tummy feel funny and then she realised it had actually been feeling a bit funny ever since she had left Granny, Dad and Aunty Blaze. She said that helping Gramps and me had felt quite **nice** and, honestly, if I could live with an ANNOYING, over-achieving little sister then surely she could TOO. So **Aunty Fury** had realised that she didn't want to be a **BADDIE** any more; she wanted to be a *goodie* and also an aunty.

BONES (the SHARK) had also declared her intention to become a *goodie* when **Aunty Fury** had explained her change of heart to all her SHARKS, so had made the **JUMP** TOO (the others all wanted to just swim about being SHARKS, which I thought was fair enough).

We all 'cheers'ed with our mugs of tea and everyone seemed **really HAPPY**. After a few tries, **Aunty Fury** actually sort of smiled and it really suited her. We decided she should stick with **Aunty Fury** as her name but that her **FURY** could now be directed at the **BADDIES**. I mean, a LOT of them really deserve it. Then the doorbell went AGAIN and I couldn't imagine who it was going to be this time . . .

BUT it turned out to be the
best visitor
EVER . . .

PIZZA!!!!!

AND
Susie and Tom.

AMAAAAAZING!

I was so **happy** to see them, and I explained to **Susie** why I hadn't answered her calls. She said to **shhh** and pass her a mug of tea, as RED had already *explained* it ALL when she had invited them over, and I *suddenly* felt a bit lucky to have such an ANNOYING busybody for a little sister.

As I watched everyone **LAUGHING** and **eating** and **chatting** round the table, I thought about how fu**n**ny *everything* is, and how it usually works out for the **BEST**, one way or another. I had thought I didn't want to be a *goodie* any more and was actually even a ***BADDIE*** for a bit, but because of all that, being a ***SUPERHERO*** – a **GOOD *SUPERHERO*** – felt MORE RIGHT than it EVER had before.

Because now I had FINALLY realised that doing the **right** thing might be **HARD**

or even **FRUSTRATING** or possibly even **INFURIATING**, I felt like I could just get on with it.

In my OWN *SUPERISH* way.

Mum leaned over and told me I was RIGHT, and then I told her, quite firmly, that even though I might be a ***goodie*** again she *absolutely*, definitely was NOT allowed to read my mind. Like, EVER.

She told me I was RIGHT about that too and she would **stop** it. And I *sort of* believed her.

After all that **KERFUFFLE** I realised that this planet belongs to all of us, so we all need to look after it as best we can. My **BEST** happens to involve jazz hands/glitter storm/**ECO COUNCILS**/interesting guitar playing and I decided, right then, to be **PROUD** to use my, erm, *unique* skills alongside all these **BRILLIANT** people, *SUPERS* and **normals** (and even secretly some *BADDIES* – I mean you, **KAPOW** and Perfecto) and SHARKS and DOGS who are also phones. Oh, and *guinea pigs* who are also *pop stars*. I thought about how everyone on this **AMAZING** planet deserves to be **saved** and how I would **save** them, even the not-so-nice ones (I mean they might come good – look at **Aunty Fury**!). Well, I would do my **BEST** and that would be enough. I would be *SUPER*.

My kind of

SUPER

anyway.

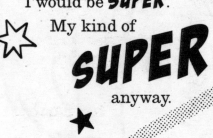

Oh, and Mum **even** said I could get a costume that FITTED now. It's almost like I have grown into my **CAPE** after all!!!!

H^m_m^m_m...

I wonder what it will be like...

The End.

TO BE CONTINUED . . .

Read all of PiZAZZ's **SUPER** ADVENTURES so far!

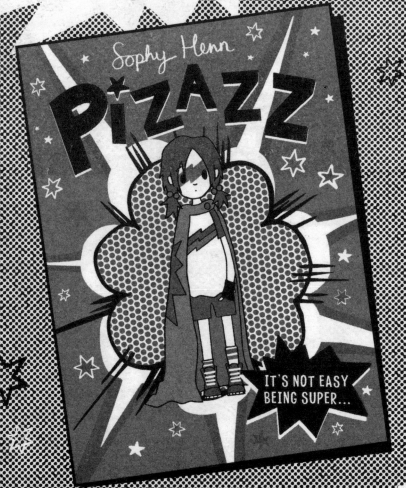

'A SPECTACULAR SUPERHERO STORY THAT FIZZES WITH FUN ON EVERY PAGE!' LIZ PICHON

Pizazz

VS Perfecto

Sophy Henn

Look out for more PIZAZZ coming soon!

Sophy Henn

is an **AWARD-WINNING**
author and illustrator with
a Masters in Illustration
from the University of Brighton. She is the
creator of the much-loved **BAD NANA** series,
the **POM POM** series, the **PIZAZZ** series, the **TED**
board book series, and the non-fiction **LIFESIZE**
series, among others. Her debut picture book
Where Bear? was nominated for the Kate
Greenaway Medal and shortlisted for the
Waterstones Children's Book Prize.

Sophy was the **WORLD BOOK DAY** illustrator in
2015 and 2016. She writes and draws in her studio
in Sussex with a large cup of tea by her side and
can't quite believe her luck!